For my Dad— "Who loves you? . . .
Nano loves you!" —K.C.

To Mom and Dad. Thank you for
everything you do! —S.L.

A FEIWEL AND FRIENDS BOOK

An imprint of Macmillan Publishing Group, LLC

120 Broadway, New York, NY 10271

Printed in China by RR Donnelley Asia Printing Solutions Ltd.,
Dongguan City, Guangdong Province.

Our books may be purchased in bulk for promotional,
educational, or business use. Please contact your local bookseller
or the Macmillan Corporate and Premium Sales
Department at (800) 221-7945 ext. 5442 or by email
at MacmillanSpecialMarkets@macmillan.com.

Library of Congress Cataloging-in-Publication Data is available.
ISBN 978-1-250-22539-9

Book design by Cindy De la Cruz

Feiwel and Friends logo designed by Filomena Tuosto

First edition, 2021

10 9 8 7 6 5 4 3 2 1

mackids.com

You Be Daddy

written by
KARLA CLARK

FEIWEL AND FRIENDS
NEW YORK

illustrated by
STEPH LEW

Daddy's too tired to be Daddy tonight.
Can you be Daddy and hug me tight?

Run my bath nice and warm?
Snuggle close if there's a storm?

Build me a bedtime fort for two?
One that fits just me and you.

Can you be Daddy and kiss me good night?
Daddy's too tired to be Daddy tonight.

He raced home from work but missed every light.

Walked in the door and had to break up a fight.

Mowed the lawn and swept the walk.

Listened to Mr. Brown talk and talk!

Grilled burgers for Maggie and hot dogs for Nick.
Played with the cat and taught her a trick.

Raced our bikes up to the park.
Played hide-and-seek until it got dark.

Can you be Daddy and turn off the light?

Daddy's too tired to be Daddy tonight.

He fixed a faucet and paid the bills.
Changed a diaper and cleaned up spills.

Played video games and shot some hoops.
Wow! He's worn out—he's really pooped!

And now he needs a great big favor.

So be a pal!
A real lifesaver!

Please be Daddy and wish me sweet dreams.

About spaceships and robots and chocolate ice cream.

Lend me your night-light and stuffed dinosaur.

Then tiptoe out and close the door.

Daddy's just too tired to stay awake.
So please be Daddy and give me a break!

What's that, kiddo? You're tired too?
You'd rather ME be Daddy instead of you?

Oh, all right then, I'll let you win.
One more big yawn . . .

and I'll be Daddy again.

For you'll always be my wonderful son.
And I'll be Daddy when the day is done.